Picnic Time

Cynthia Rider • Alex Brychta

OXFORD

UNIVERSITY PRESS

"Picnic time!" said Dad.

Biff sat on a log.

Some sheep came.

8

"Run!" said Kipper.

They sat on a bridge.

Some ducks came.

12

"Run!" said Chip.

They sat on a wall.

Some donkeys came.

"Run!" said Biff.

They sat on a rock.

Oh no! The rain came!

Think about the story

What happened when Biff gave the duck some bread?

Why did the children run away from the animals?

Where was the picnic? How do you know?

What food would you like to take on a picnic?

Tangled lines

Who will get the picnic?